Temple (

CU00842962

Between passion and pain

by

Pablo Criscito

Copyright 2013, Pablo Criscito

Author's edition, Frankfurt (Main), Germany

On the path to being,

we must pass through

the experience of pain.

Content

Lady Anna

The door-bell rang. Lady Anna in her black latex mini dress and high-heels went gracefully to the inter phone.
“Hello?”, she called into the handset in her firm voice.
“Hello mistress. It’s John here”.
“Enter, slave. Brace yourself!”, Lady Anna ordered her devoted slave.
She opened the door. John was a civil servant about the age of fifty. None of his friends or colleagues knew that he spent much of his spare time with Lady Anna. John loved being humiliated. He needed the pain. John stepped into the temple-like building, in which five dominatrices reigned supreme, day and night.
“Change your clothes in the cabin, you little shit!”
John went into the cabin and removed his suit, his shirt and his socks. He

wore a black leather thong under the suit.
“Come on, you piece of shit. Sit down in the confessional and tell me all the bad things you’ve done since the last time, and beg me for mercy!", shouted Lady Anna.
The slave went into the double cabin confessional and sat down trembling with excitement. The dominatrix went into the other cabin.
“Talk to me, you rotten bastard!”
“I committed insurance fraud."
“I am sure, that‘s not all. Speak!”
“I lied to my daughter." That’s all.”
“Now ask for forgiveness, you dirty motherfucker!”
“Mistress, please forgive me!”
“You will receive two lessons. Get out of the cabin!”
Lady Anna went to a platform and took the pony head harness.
“Sit down on the slave chair!”

The civil servant maintained a timid silence, although he was enjoying the situation thoroughly. He loved the kick he got out of serving Lady Anna.
The dominatrix put the pony head harness on John, complete with bit and lead.
“Open your mouth and bite down on the bit, limp dick!"
John did as Lady Anna commanded.
"Your breath stinks. Next time brush your teeth! Obey, slave!”
“Yes, mistress.”
The dominatrix went to a commode and fetched a long steel chain, clipping it to the pony head harness.
“Down on all fours, you sorry ass piece of shit!”
The slave obeyed.
The dominatrix led the civil servant around the room on the chain, beat him hard with a riding crop and insulting him over and over. Lady

Anna's voice thrilled John like nothing else.
"I've got more pain in store for you, slave!"
Lady Anna removed the pony head harness, dressed John in a leather mask with a mouth opening and fetched the mouth gag.
"Sit back down on the slave chair!"
John went and sat down submissively on the slave chair.
"Open your mouth wide!"
Lady Ann pushed the mouth gag into the slave's mouth and stretched it to 3 inches wide.
John's eye widened in agony as his mouth was stretched.
Next, the dominatrix handcuffed him.
Completely helpless, John on the slave chair and enjoyed every moment of the pain.
After half an hour, Lady Anna went to her slave, pulled the mouth gag out of

his mouth, and removed the leather mask and the handcuffs.
“Get dressed in the cabin and then get out of my sight. I expect to see you back here in three days!”, said the dominatrix, nodding her dismissal.
“Yes, mistress.”
The sufferer got dressed hastily, and left the house.

Lady Laura

27 year old dominatrix Lady Laura with her full dark hair, sat on her designer couch in her black leather trousers and red corset, waiting impatiently for her slave, who was late.
Suddenly, the doorbell rang. Lady Laura opened it.
Peter stepped into the room and fell instantly to his knees before the dominatrix.
"Mistress! Forgive me, I am unworthy of you, I was late. But I could not do anything about it."
"Shut up, slave! Today, your torture will be all the worse. You will never forget this day. Stand up and go and strip in the cabin!"
The 32 year old manager went to take off his clothes, stepping out of the cabin naked a moment later.
"Go and stand facing the St. Andrew's Cross," ordered Lady Laura sternly.

The slave obeyed meekly.
The dominatrix secured Peter to the the St. Andrew's Cross using the hand and foot manacles and then took up the leather lash. The manager loved the pain - he needed the torture to be happy.
Lady Laura brought the leather lash down forcefully on Peter's back and legs, drawing blood more than once, which dripped from his skin. In this torture, Peter moaned with pleasure.
Again and again, the dominatrix whipped her charge.
“Have you had enough?”, asked Lady Laura.
“Yes, mistress.”
“We are not through yet! Your suffering isn't over! Go to the rack!”
The dominatrix fetched a leather mask and put it on her slave.
“Lie down with your back on the rack.”
Lady Laura secured Peter's hands and feet to the rack and began to stretch

him. The manager's face was strained with pain. The agony of the rack made him scream out loud.

After ten minutes, Lady Laura finished her work and opened the slave's manacles.

"Take a shower and get dressed. Then get out of here. I will see you again!"

"Yes, my mistress."

The ice-cold dominatrix vanished into another room, while her slave still savored the pain that ravaged his back, his arms, and his legs. Peter's pain would linger long after he left his mistress – just as he wanted it to. Lady Laura always did a perfect job, and he had already been visiting her regularly for three years. Twenty minutes later, Lady Laura heard the entrance door close. She was ready for the next customer.

Lady Hanna

Lady Hanna, a mature red-headed Amazonian, opened the entrance door, the moment, the bell rang. The dominatrix wore a black wrapped patent leather mini skirt, a black corset and red high-heels.

Anthony entered the studio. The dominatrix nodded graciously to him.

“See this, you dirty bastard? You’ll feel it in full force today!”, she announced to him, showing him her leather strap.

“Go to the cabin and take off your clothes!”

Anthony obeyed wordlessly.

The 45 years old stock broker came back in a black studded thong.

“Sit down on the punishment block!”

He complied.

Lady Hanna took up the leather strap and beat Anthony hard. He moaned with joy. The pain was the most important thing in his life. Only in pain did he feel human.

Five minutes later, the dominatrix stopped the pain and Anthony left the punishment block, fully satisfied.

“Mistress, may I express one wish?

“Speak, slave!”

“I would like to drink your warm golden shower. Would you please grant me this wish?"

“Okay, slave, I will allow it.”

The dominatrix strapped a funnel head harness onto Anthony’s head, vanished for a while and came back with a bottle of golden shower, finding stock broker already waiting on the slave chair.

Lady Hanna slowly poured the warm golden shower into the funnel. The slave swallowed obediently.

After the man had drunk every drop of the golden shower, his mistress removed the funnel head harness. Next, she fitted the stock broker with a leather mask and hung him up by his using two feet suspension cuffs. The man hung completely helpless in the room.

"Slave, do you know, what you're in for?"

"No, mistress. But you promised me a lot of pain."

Lady Hanna went to the cabinet and got four candles and a lighter. She lit the candles, waited for a while and then dripped the hot wax all over the stock broker's back and thighs.

Slowly, the hot wax trickled across on the slave's body. Anthony grimaced, but he enjoyed every moment of the pain.

Once all four candles had been used up, the dominatrix ordered her slave to get dressed and leave.

The visit was an unforgettable experience for Anthony.

Lady Monique

Black-haired Lady Monique wore a patent leather mini dress and high heels as she opened the door to Mike. The man entered the studio.

“Slave, are you ready?”

“Yes, mistress.”

Minutes later, Mike was naked and ready for today's lesson.

Lady Monique put a leather neckband around his neck, on which was a leading ring. She threaded a long steel chain through the ring and pulled the slave into a jail cell. She tied up his arms to the steel rings that hung on the wall. Mike sat on a slave chair in his cell.

The exigent Lady Monique, a renowned dominatrix in the city, fetched the foot manacles, which were attached to an extension bar, and fastened the manacles on Mike.

Fitness trainer Mike's face contorted in pain.
"When I am allowed to get out my cell?", he asked quietly.
"Shut up, slave! You will be here until tomorrow morning. Your pain will last the whole night. You have earned it!"
After this, the dominatrix closed the cell door with a loud bang. The cell was a bare room with stone walls and no toilet.
The submissive Mike enjoyed every minute of his captivity. He loved Lady Monique. She was the only mistress he had ever had. His legs, stretched by the extension bar, were aching. He had hardly ever experienced such a strong pain.
Around 4:00 in the morning, the cell door opened suddenly. Lady Monique gave her prisoner a drink of water and held a harness with a butterfly gag in her hand. She put the harness on her

slave, pushed the gag into his mouth and pumped it up.

Once she had finished, she left the cell, banging the door loudly behind her.

The next morning, the dominatrix set her slave free and bade him goodbye. Mike was deeply satisfied, although his mouth and his legs ached. He was sure to come back.

Lady Viola

Lady Viola was famous for her excellent electrotherapy. Today, Gerry was able to enjoy this special treatment. The charming man presented Lady Viola a large bouquet of roses.
Expectantly, the 66 years old pensioner sat on the slave chair in his black thong and watched Lady Viola. She plugged in her instruments of torture. The dominatrix wore a patent leather mini skirt and a dark blue corset.
“Take off your thong, slave!”, ordered Lady Viola with stern voice.
Gerry obeyed and put the thong on a small platform.
Deftly, the dominatrix put the electric shock cock ring on the elderly man and switched on the power.
The power flowed and the pensioner felt the strong pain it caused to his

penis. Gerry closed his eyes, reveling in the discomfort. The treatment continued for about one hour. Again and again, he raised his arms, moving them as though he were conducting an orchestra, delighting in the agony.

Afterwards this, Lady Viola went to the pensioner and placed two magnetic pain balls on his nipples. The elderly man moaned with pleasure. He adored the pain.

The dominatrix fetched an electro shocker, tuned it on a middle level and gave the pensioner electric shocks on his back, chest, arms and legs. The man loved the treatment. Pain was his life.

After two hours, Gerry put on his clothes, said goodbye and left Lady Viola's studio, highly satisfied.

Printed in Great Britain
by Amazon.co.uk, Ltd.,
Marston Gate.